S. Claus – The Tr[illegible]

Tom knew it was goi[illegible] Eve as soon as he looked [illegible] window, not long after Mum went out to do some last minute Christmas shopping. There was a deer in the back garden . . .

S. Claus – The Truth!

Andrew Matthews
Illustrated by Tony Ross

MAMMOTH

First published in Great Britain 1989 by Mammoth
an imprint of Mandarin Paperbacks
Michelin House, 81 Fulham Road, London SW3 6RB
Mandarin is an imprint of the
Octopus Publishing Group

The story 'S. Claus – The Truth!'
first appeared in Stuff and Nonsense magazine
November 1988

ISBN 0 7497 0085 8

A CIP Catalogue record is available for this title
from the British Library.

Printed in Great Britain by Cox and Wyman, Reading

CONTENTS

Also by Andrew Matthews

WOLF PIE
DIXIE'S DEMON
THE QUIET PIRATE

For Mum and Dad and many Christmasses

S. Claus – The Truth!

Tom knew it was going to be an unusual Christmas Eve as soon as he looked through the kitchen window, not long after Mum went out to do some last-minute Christmas shopping. There was a deer in the back garden. An antlered head appeared round the branches of a rose bush and looked straight at him. At least, Tom *thought* it was looking straight at him – it was difficult to tell because the deer was wearing sunglasses.

Tom opened the kitchen door and stood on the back step, staring. The deer ducked its head, shifted its feet and said, "Oppit, kid!'

'What?' gasped Tom.

'You 'eard me! 'Oppit!' snapped the deer. 'You're makin' me dead nervous, standin' there gawpin'!'

Tom broddled his ears with a little finger, closed his eyes tight and counted to ten. When he opened his eyes, the deer was still there.

'You're a talking deer!' he cried.

'Well I never!' said the deer sarcastically. 'Go to the top of the class! Just leave me alone, will yer? I've 'ad a long journey an' I'm knackered!'

'What are you doing in our garden?' asked Tom.

'No peace for the wicked, is there?' grumbled the deer. 'I'm 'avin' a rest in your garden, 'cos I just arrived from Lapland, right? An' before you ask, I came 'ere to get away . . . from 'im!'

'Him?' frowned Tom.

'S. Claus!' whispered the deer.

It was then that Tom noticed the deer's nose for the first time. It was the colour of a ripe tomato.

'Is your name Rudolph?' he enquired.

'Too right, mate!' replied the deer.

''Ow did you know?'

'Your red nose.'

Rudolf snorted angrily and stamped his back legs. 'My nose ain't red! It's flamingo pink!'

'Sorry!' Tom apologised. 'But, why do you want to get away from Santa Claus? I always thought he was a kindly, cheery sort of person.'

'Hah!' scoffed Rudolf. 'Let me tell you the truth about S. Claus, my son! That blokey is well round the twist! Every Christmas Eve we spend all night bombin' round the world, clatterin' about on people's roofs . . . an' for what?'

'Er . . . well,' said Tom, 'to take presents to all the girls and boys, I suppose.'

'Oh yeah?' sneered Rudolf. 'Who gives you your presents, then?'

'My mum and dad, actually,' confessed Tom. 'I woke up last year while they were putting toys on my bed.'

'It's the same all over the world!' said Rudolf. 'Every 'ouse we go to, the parents 'ave beaten us to it! We end up cartin' a sleighful o' toys all the way back to Lapland!'

'Poor Santa!' exclaimed Tom. 'He must feel really miserable.'

'No chance, mate! It's ho-ho-ho all the time with that geezer! 'E's so cheerful it gets right up my nostrils! This year I decided that enough was enough. I took one look at the ice an' snow outside the stable door an' I thought "knickers!". I mean to get some serious partyin' done this Yule! Where do reindeer boogie on down round 'ere?'

Tom thought hard.

'To be honest, I don't know,' he said at last. 'There's a pub in town called "The Stag's Head", but I haven't seen any stags going in there.'

'Strewth!' groaned Rudolph. ''Ow about showin' me the sights, then? It'll make a change from Lapland, there's only ice an' snow to look at there!'

'W-e-e-l-l . . .' said Tom.

'Go on, be a mate!'

'It's quite a long walk,' said Tom, making excuses.

'No problem!' said Rudolph breezily. 'Jump on me back an' we'll fly there!'

Tom seemed to have been talked into something there was no way out of. He climbed up on the reindeer's back and put his arms around its neck.

'Rudolph,' he asked curiously, 'why are you wearing sunglasses?'

'I wanna disguise meself, don't I?' Rudolph replied. 'You 'angin' on tight? 'Ere we go-o-o-o!'

And they flew.

They landed in a supermarket car park just around the corner from the shopping precinct. No one noticed. Everybody was so busy with their Christmas shopping that when Tom led Rudolph into the precinct square, not a head turned to look.

There was a big Christmas tree in the square, surrounded by loudspeakers blaring out carols about peace and rejoicing. The people bustling didn't look very peaceful or joyful; they looked hassled.

'Is this it?' whined Rudolph. 'Just a lot o' people runnin' in an' out o' shops?'

'Um, yes,' said Tom. 'Christmas is a busy time. There's buying presents and wrapping them. Then, tomorrow, people will spend a lot of time cooking Christmas dinner, unwrapping presents, clearing up and washing up. Mum usually vacuums the front room carpet because the Christmas tree keeps shedding needles.'

'You're kiddin'!' croaked Rudolph. 'I thought people looked forward to Christmas Day!'

'They do.'

'S. Claus ain't the only one 'oo's bonkers!' muttered Rudolph.

Tom and Rudolph walked around the precinct looking in the shop windows. Rudolph grew gloomier by the minute. His mood was not improved by the butcher's window.

'Strike a light!' he squealed. 'What's this lot?'

'They're turkeys,' Tom said.

'And what's that stuff over there?'

'That's a side of venison,' blushed Tom.

'Oh, be'ave!' breathed Rudolph. 'That's a bit out of order, ain't it?'

Tom was saved from having to say anything by a little blonde girl wearing a blue coat. She was holding a ten pence piece. She walked all around Rudolph, frowned, then approached Tom and said, 'Where do I put the money in?'

'You can't put money in him,' Tom explained. 'He's a real reindeer.'

'I want to wide him!' said the girl. 'I want to wide the weindeer!'

'I don't think he'd like it!' said Tom hurriedly.

'I want to wide him!' the girl insisted.

'Yes, but – '

'I WANT TO WIDE THE WEINDEER WIGHT AWAY!' screamed the girl.

Rudolph bowed his head and looked at her over the top of his sunglasses.

'If you don't buzz off quick, Goldilocks,' he growled. 'I'm gonna bite you on the bum!'

The little girl's mouth and eyes opened wide.

'Mummy!' she squealed, and darted off into the crowds.

At that moment, the loudspeakers around the Christmas tree spluttered in the middle of 'Silent Night' and started playing 'Jingle Bells'. A large sleigh made its way across

the precinct, drawn by eleven reindeer. In the driving seat, a large, familiar figure with red robes and a long white beard boomed out, 'Ho, Ho, ho!' to the astonished shoppers.

'That's peculiar!' said Tom. 'I thought the Christmas parade was cancelled this year.'

'It ain't a parade!' moaned Rudolph. 'It's 'im! It's my guv'ner!'

The sleigh halted right in front of them.

'Ho, ho, ho!' thundered S. Claus.

'Wotcha, chief!' said Rudolph feebly. ''Ow's tricks?'

S. Claus held his sides and burst into peals of laughter.

'See what I mean about cheerful?' Rudolph muttered to Tom out of the side of his mouth.

'You've led me a pretty dance, Rudolph my boy,' S. Claus said at length, wiping tears from his eyes with a red-gloved finger, 'but it's time to get back to work. We're off to China!'

'China?' yelped Rudolph. 'But, chief, they don't celebrate Christmas in China!'

'It'll be a surprise for them, won't it?' chuckled S. Claus.

'Just a minute!' shouted a new voice. 'What's the big idea?'

A man was approaching the sleigh. He was dressed as Father Christmas and he looked cross.

'What's going on?' he shouted. 'I'm Father Christmas round here! I've got a grotto over in Barrington's Toys!'

'My dear sir – !' spluttered S. Claus.

'I'm going to complain to the Father Christmas Union about this!' roared the man.

'And what about my Primrose?' demanded another voice. A thin-faced woman pushed her way through the crowd that had gathered, dragging with her the little blonde girl, who was still bawling loudly.

'Your animal was rude to my Primrose! You can't bring talking reindeer here and let them wander about insulting innocent children!'

Rudolph caught sight of a policeman coming towards them. 'Chief!' he hissed. 'I reckon we oughter bottle out and scarper before the Old Bill arrive!'

'Good thinking!' agreed S. Claus. 'You get into your harness, I'll try to calm things down a bit!' He beamed at the woman. 'Ho, ho, ho! A merry Christmas to you!'

'Right!' snapped the Barrington's Toys' Father Christmas, rolling up his sleeves. 'That does it! Step out of that sleigh and settle it like a man, you fat fraud!'

'Er . . . ho, ho, ho!' said S. Claus, looking worried. 'Peace and goodwill to all!'

'Go for it, Sant!' yelled Rudolph as he slipped his muzzle through a noseband.

The reindeer gathered their back legs and

leapt up into the sky, carrying the sleigh with them and leaving behind the faint echoes of S. Claus's final, 'Ho, ho, ho!'

On Christmas morning, Tom's mum found a mysterious parcel for Tom on the front doorstep. In it were a splendid flamingo pink sweater and a card inscribed, 'From your friend in Lapland.'

'Lapland?' laughed Mum. 'I didn't know you had a friend in Lapland!'

Well I do,' said Tom. 'A very dear friend!'

Billy's Big Break

Christmas was a busy time at Duckworth End Juniors. There were murals to be painted, decorations to be made and put up round the place, cards to be drawn and carols to be learned. Most important of all, there were the rehearsals for the Nativity play.

This was a major production, involving pupils from all classes and most of the teachers, who did things like make-up, lighting and something mysterious called 'Front of House'. This did not turn out to be as mysterious as it sounded. It meant putting out all the chairs in the hall in neat rows, counting them, moving them around and counting them again.

The play was being directed by Mrs Golightly, who didn't go lightly because she was a plump, cheerful lady with grey hair and twinkling eyes. At least, she started off being cheerful and twinkle-eyed; as the day of the performance drew nearer, her face wore a worried look and her eyes were underlined with dark half-moons.

Most of her trouble was down to Billy Houndsome in 2E. Billy had sweet, innocent looks and a good, loud voice. Unfortunately, Billy wasn't as sweet and innocent as he looked and his memory was like a tea bag – anything that was put into it leaked out through a thousand holes. Inspiration came to Mrs Golightly like a blow from a blacksmith's hammer. Billy could play the part of Joseph! That meant he could stand around looking sweet and innocent until he said his only line, 'Is there any room at the inn?' Mrs Golightly was sure that even Billy could cope with seven short words.

The trouble started in the very first rehearsal. All went well until the visit of the Three Wise Men to the stable.

'I bring the new king gold!' announced the First Wise Man.

'And I bring him Frankenstein!' said the Second.

'Eric?' said Mrs Golightly in her kind aunt's voice. 'I think if you read your script ever so carefully, you'll find that the word is frankincense. Carry on, Third Wise man!'

'And – I – ,' said the Third Wise Man, holding a trembling script right up in front of his face, 'bring him . . . er . . . um . . . murry-huh-huh . . . er . . . myrahuh?'

'That's myrrh, Jonathan,' said Mrs Golightly.

While this conversation was going on, the Holy Family was muttering angrily to itself around the crib. It continued while the Third Wise Man tried his speech again, and when he finished a full-scale tussle broke out between Billy Houndsome and Lillian Wu, who was playing Mary.

'Haven't!' shrieked Lillian, trying to pull Billy's hair.

''Ave, 'ave, 'ave!' shouted Billy.

He ducked away from Lillian's grasping fingers and knocked over the crib. The battered old doll playing the baby Jesus rolled across the stage and got even more battered.

'Now then!' barked Mrs Golightly in her teacher's voice. 'What seems to be the trouble?'

Lillian drew in a deep breath and spoke like an express train.

'It's Billy Houndsome! He's horrible! He keeps saying I've got a big bot and I haven't but he keeps saying it and he's mean and awful and I hate him and I don't want to be Mary if he's going to be Joseph!'

'Well she *'as* got a big bot, ain't she, miss?' yelled Billy. 'She keeps bumpin' me with it! Nearly 'ad me over a coupla times!'

'Be quiet, both of you!' roared Mrs Golightly.

'But, miss – ' protested Billy.

'I said, be quiet! Billy, pick up the crib! Lillian, pick up the doll and wrap it up in its swaddling clothes!'

Quivering with sobs, Lillian walked over to the doll and lifted it from the stage.

'Ma-ma!' said the doll and its right leg clattered to the floor.

Mrs Golightly made changes in the cast. Ronald Reeves from 1N was promoted from Second Shepherd to Joseph. He was a lot shorter than Lillian, it was true, and his spectacles looked as though they were made out of the bottoms of milk bottles, but

Mrs Golightly thought that no one would notice as long as he wore a really big headcloth.

Billy took Ronald's place. Mrs Golightly knew he would never get his line – 'Lo, what star is that shining yonder in the East?' – completely right, but he could probably get quite close if he practised enough.

Billy's first stab at his new role was not promising. When his turn came, he grabbed the First Shepherd by the arm, squinted up at the ceiling and said cheerily, 'Blimey! Cop a whack o' that lot up there, mate! Is that a UFO, or what?'

'Billy!' called Mrs Golightly with a pained expression. 'I don't think you've quite mastered your words yet, have you?'

'Not yet, miss,' Billy admitted. 'I didn't understand what they meant, so I got me dad to explain 'em. I reckon what 'e told me, like, makes more sense.'

'It doesn't have to make sense, Billy!' snapped Mrs Golightly. 'It's a Nativity play! Besides, the audience will understand it, even if you don't!'

'My grandad won't for a start, miss!' chuckled Billy. ''E's deaf as a post!'

The rest of the rehearsal went quite smoothly, until Mrs Golightly noticed the tinies, who were playing the shepherds' flock of sheep. They were gathering around Billy in a tight knot. Some were smiling, some were frowning and some were stamping their feet in angry frustration. Suddenly, Billy's voice boomed out triumphantly, 'Snap! I win!'

'Billy Houndsome!' screeched Mrs Golightly in her fire-breathing dragon's voice. 'What on earth do you think you're playing at?'

Billy emerged from the tinies, clutching

an untidy pile of cards.

'Snap, miss,' he said. 'They can't play Pontoon. They keep gettin' the addin' up wrong!'

'Billy Houndsome,' seethed Mrs Golightly, 'you are out of this Nativity play! Definitely, absolutely and finally OUT!'

'OK miss!' said Billy happily. 'You're the boss!'

With Billy definitely, absolutely and finally out of the Nativity play, everything went brilliantly. For a week, Mrs Golightly went about smiling. She told the head teacher that this year's play would be the best yet.

And then flu arrived at Duckworth End.

Several sheep and both shepherds went down with it. The rest of the cast had such streaming eyes and runny noses that Mrs Golightly thought it might be more appropriate to put on Noah's Flood. Two of the sheep became shepherds and apart from being so nervous that they had to dash to the loos every five minutes, the tinies coped remarkably well.

And then, the week before the performance, the Angel of the Lord caught flu.

Mrs Golightly went to see the head teacher in despair.

'I don't know what to do!' she whimpered. 'There's nobody left with a voice loud enough to play the Angel!'

'I can think of one good, loud voice you're not using,' the head said helpfully.

'You don't mean . . . ?' whispered Mrs Golightly.

'Billy Houndsome,' said the head. 'The only alternative would be to cancel the whole thing. This school has put on a Nativity play every Christmas since it was opened. Be a pity to break that tradition because of one unruly boy.'

'Billy's not an unruly boy!' croaked Mrs Golightly. 'He's a volcano! He's a hurricane! He's a natural disaster!'

So, with a week to go, Billy was most definitely, absolutely and finally back in the Nativity play. He came to rehearsals, read his lines out clearly and didn't play cards or argue with other members of the cast. Only one thing troubled Mrs Golightly.

'Billy,' she said, 'you will learn your lines, won't you?'

'I'll do me best, miss!' Billy said obligingly. 'Me dad's explained what it all means, so I got it straight!'

'I hope so!' murmured Mrs Golightly.

The dress rehearsal of the play was really promising. Ronald Reeves was given such a bushy stage beard that his face hardly showed. One of the tinies brought a Superman tea towel for a headcloth and the leg kept on falling off the doll, but otherwise there were no real hitches.

Billy was the star of the show. In his flowing white robes and halo (a bent wire coat hanger painted gold) he looked angelic and much to Mrs Golightly's delight he was word-perfect.

'I'm so pleased with you, Billy!' she said to him afterwards in her sunshine voice. 'How did you manage to learn your lines in the end?'

'I didn't, miss!' grinned Billy. 'I got 'em written down on me 'ands!'

Billy held out his open palms. They looked as if spiders had been writing on them in blue biro.

*

On the night of the performance, the cast kept peeping into the hall. As it was filled with people, they grew more and more excited. The atmosphere in the dressing room was like the inside of a can of fizzy drink that had been well shaken.

'Settle down!' urged Mrs Golightly in her king cobra's voice. 'If you run around, you'll get hot and sweaty and your make-up will run!'

Even as she spoke, Mrs Golightly heard the muffled strains of the school choir singing 'Once in Royal David's city'.

'Right!' she whispered loudly. 'Places, everyone!'

As he passed her on his way to the back of the stage, Mrs Golightly noticed a shiny band of sweat on Billy's forehead. She mopped him with a tissue.

'How are you feeling, Billy?'

'Dead weird, miss. My insides feel like there's a disco goin' on in 'em!'

The back of the stage was hot and stuffy. Billy wiggled in his robes as cold worms of sweat slithered down his back. After what seemed hours, he heard his cue and stepped through a gap in the curtains into a circle of white light.

The audience gave an 'oh-isn't-he-sweet' gasp.

Billy took a deep breath, glanced at his hands – and a shock of panic went through him. His palms had been sweating so much that nothing was left of his lines but a blue smear.

Billy's mind went completely blank.

The shepherds went down on their knees, shielding their eyes from the light.

'Who art thou?' piped the First Shepherd. 'For I am sore afraid!'

Billy blinked desperately.

'Er . . . fear not!' he said. 'Er . . . don't be scared, like! I gotta bit o' good news for you, 'aven't I? See, this baby's just been born, an' 'e's a real cracker! If I was you, I'd nip down the local pub an' 'ave a quick butchers. You'll find 'im out the back!'

Billy's speech was followed by a most peculiar silence, and then the choir went into, 'O, come, all ye faithful'.

The following morning, the head teacher sent for Mrs Golightly. As soon as she stepped into his study, she started talking.

'I know! You don't have to tell me what a disaster the play was! It wasn't really Billy's fault, he did his best! I blame myself. I should have known better!'

To her surprise, the head grinned broadly.

'As a matter of fact, I wanted to congratulate you! I thought Billy's performance was very original. Actually, he's given me an idea.'

'Oh?' gulped Mrs Golightly.

'Children do find the words of the Bible rather difficult to understand,' the head explained. 'I thought, next year, we might do a sort of bang-up-to-date Nativity play. I was wondering if young Billy Houndsome might write the script for it.'

Mrs Golightly was stunned. She put a hand up to her face and muttered, 'Cop a whack of that lot up there, mate! Is that a UFO, or what?'

'Are you feeling quite all right?' enquired the head.

'Yes, fine!' said Mrs Golightly.

'I think Billy's version of the Nativity play might be a refreshing change. Something new, something different!'

'Oh,' Mrs Golightly laughed weakly, 'it'll be different all right!'

Sir Darryl and the Hag of Horror Mountain

It was Christmas at Camelot. The halls were hung with branches of holly and all the knights of the Round Table had gathered to make merry. King Arthur listened contentedly as, one by one, his brave knights described the jousts they had won and the evil giants and ferocious dragons they had fought.

And then came Sir Darryl's turn.

Sir Darryl was a newly-made knight. He was thin, with red hair and looked rather nervous. When he realised that everyone in the Banqueting Hall was staring at him expectantly, he blushed redder than a holly berry.

'Come, brave Sir Darryl!' said King Arthur in a kindly voice. 'Do not be modest! Tell all the Round Table, here gathered, what stirring adventures you have had! For nothing pleases us more than the yarn of a newly-made knight facing perils to win his spurs!'

'Well, my liege,' said Sir Darryl reluctantly, 'I helped a fair young maiden in distress last week.'

'What manner of fair young maiden?' cried King Arthur. 'And what was her distress?'

'Um . . . she wasn't exactly fair,' admitted Sir Darryl, 'and she wasn't very young. In fact, she was an old widow woman. I had to rescue her Jack.'

'I see!' smiled King Arthur. 'Jack is her only son, I suppose?'

'No, my liege,' mumbled Sir Darryl. 'Jack is her cat. He was stuck up an apple tree. I got a ladder and brought him down. But I did it all by myself! And it was ever so cold, my hands went quite blue . . .' His voice died to a dry whisper as he saw the astonished faces all around him.

'Is that all!' gasped the King.

'It's not my fault, my liege!' complained Sir Darryl. 'All the other knights had bagged the best bits! I was going to have a go at the Ogmore Ogre, but Sir Bevedere beat me to it! And I set out to slay the Warwick Worm, but I lost my way and by the time I got there, Sir Gavin had already slain the monster and the local villagers were roasting an ox in his honour!'

'Just a minute!' said Sir Lancelot from the other side of the table. 'The last time I saw you, you were off to put paid to the Awkward Witch of Oxford. What happened?'

'She turned me into a newt!' said Sir Darryl miserably. 'It took Merlin three days to change me back to human form. I went back to Oxford, but the witch had flown off to France for her Christmas holiday!'

'My liege!' Sir Lancelot called out. 'Sir Darryl's valour is not yet proved! It is for you to send him on a quest fraught with danger!'

'Aye!' cried the other knights.

King Arthur frowned and tugged his beard, deep in thought.

'Let Merlin be brought to me!' he said at last. 'I will seek his advice on – '

Before the King had a chance to finish, there was a bright green flash and Merlin the wizard stood before him, bowing low.

'You called, sire?' he said.

'Yes, Merlin. I need to send young Sir Darryl on a quest at once and it had better be a tricky one because the other knights are starting to talk.'

'I shall consult the Great Book of Quests!' announced Merlin. He waved his hands and a large red book appeared in them.

'How about a nice, juicy giant?' suggested King Arthur.

'Alas, sire,' Merlin replied, leafing through the book, 'all the giants are spoken for up to the end of March.'

'An evil knight, then!' said King Arthur. 'Nothing like a ding-dong battle with a really wicked varlet to get a young knight's career off to a good start!'

'Sir Kay vanquished the very last evil knight in November, sire,' said Merlin.

'Pikestaffs and odd-bodkins!' exclaimed King Arthur. 'Is there nothing in the book? If this kingdom gets too peaceful, there won't be anything for us to do!'

Merlin's face grew dark and serious. Blue

sparks fizzed out of his beard and crackled on the flagstones at his feet.

'There is one quest that is vacant, sire!' he said. 'You have not yet sent any knight to deal with . . . the Hag of Horror Mountain!'

'The Hag of Horror Mountain!' hissed the knights, turning pale.

'The H-hag of Horror Mountain?' gulped Sir Darryl. 'What's she like?'

'Oh, you know!' said Sir Lancelot. 'Evil-minded, cruel, vicious, uses the powers of darkness to wreak havoc. Usual sort of thing for a hag.'

King Arthur stood up solemnly.

'So be it!' he proclaimed. 'Sir Darryl, you are to set out immediately on your quest. You will travel to Horror Mountain. You will face unknown dangers and unspeakable terrors. You must vanquish the Hag, or perish in the attempt! Oh, yes, and by the way, a merry Christmas to you!'

'Thank you, my liege!' croaked Sir Darryl.

Sir Darryl called on Dirk, his trusty squire, to help him get ready. Dirk saddled Dandy, Sir Darryl's horse, and packed his saddle-bags with provisions. After that, he helped Sir Darryl on with his armour.

'You know, Dirk,' said Sir Darryl as the squire strapped him into his breastplate, 'with all these unknown dangers and unspeakable terrors to face on my quest, I'm really glad you'll be there! If I was on my own, I think I'd be a little nervous! But with you beside me to cheer me up, I'm sure I'll be as valorous as anything!'

'Er . . . actually, I wanted to 'ave a word with you about the quest, my lord,' said Dirk.

'Speak freely, trusty Dirk!' cried Sir Darryl.

'Er . . . actually, I'm not comin' with you, my lord,' said Dirk. 'It bein' Christmas an' that, me mum won't let me go.'

'Your mum?' shrieked Sir Darryl.

'She says no way am I goin'! She's gone to a lotta trouble this Yule. Gotta goose, apple sauce, quince puddin's, the lot! She says if I'm not sat round the table for me Christmas dinner, she'll do 'er nut!' Dirk sniffed apologetically. 'I'm dead sorry, my lord, but you know what me mum's like! We've both got our duties to do.'

'Yes!' agreed Sir Darryl. 'My duty is to ride through the winter wilderness in search of the Hag of Horror Mountain and your duty is to stuff yourself full of roast goose and quince pudding!'

'A man's gotta do what a man's gotta do, my lord!' sighed Dirk.

Old legends tell how, at Camelot, it was eternally summer. What they don't tell is how, that winter, it was bitterly cold everywhere else. Albion, as the land was known then, was held fast in the grasp of snow

and ice. Sir Darryl's armour let in every freezing blast of wind and, by the end of the first morning, he had caught a cold. He spent the first night of his quest in a village stable with Dandy. The stable-keeper was a friendly sort of chap and chatted with Sir Darryl for a while.

'You'm on a quest, then!' he said.

'How did you know?' asked Sir Darryl.

'You'm goin' to bed with your armour on!' explained the stable-keeper.

'I'm seeking the Hag of Horror Mountain,' said Sir Darryl. 'What's the best road to take?'

A look of terror crossed the stable-keeper's honest features.

'Follow the road through the Valley of Desolation,' he said uneasily, 'then turn left at the mouldy gibbet. You can't miss 'Orror Mountain! Terrible big thing, all covered with boulders! But look 'ere, take my advice and don't 'ave no truck with 'ags! Fearsome things, they be, and I do 'ear tell as 'ow the 'Ag of 'Orror Mountain be the most fearsome 'ag of all!'

As he spoke, the wind began to howl and an owl hooted in the darkness outside the stable.

'I can't back down now!' said Sir Darryl. 'I'm a newly-made knight, you see, and I've yet to win my spurs.'

'Spurs?' said the stable-keeper darkly. 'You'll be lucky if there's enough left of you to wear spurs! I bid you good night, good knight . . . and pleasant dreams!'

The next morning was Christmas Eve. Sir Darryl set off before it was light. When day finally broke, he found himself in the Valley of Desolation. Nothing grew there. The sides of the valley were bare and rocky. There wasn't even a sparrow or a crow for company. Dandy plodded between drifts of snow that were whiter than bleached bones.

Sir Darryl reached Horror Mountain just after noon. It was a ghastly tower of black granite. Reluctantly, the newly-made knight dismounted and patted Dandy's muzzle.

'You can't climb up there, old friend,' he said. 'If I'm not back by nightfall, return to the stable in the village. I'm sure the stable-keeper will take good care of you.'

Then Sir Darryl strapped on his sharpest sword, took up his best shield and set off up the lower slopes of Horror Mountain. Wind moaned around the black boulders and a few flakes of snow fell. With each step, the way grew steeper and Sir Darryl's armour seemed to grow heavier and heavier.

'This is no good!' he told himself. 'I'll wear myself out at this rate!' He opened the visor on his helmet and shouted, 'Hag?

Show yourself! I am brave Sir Darryl and the goodly King Arthur has sent me on a quest to vanquish you!'

No sooner were the words out of his mouth, than a peal of thunder rolled in the mountain. A bolt of lightning flickered like a snake's tongue and where it struck the ground not far from Sir Darryl, the Hag appeared out of the cold air.

She looked wild. Her face was grimy and her hair, streaming in the wind, was tangled and knotty. Her eyes were blue and fierce. She raised a filthy hand and pointed at the knight, the ragged sleeve of her black robe flapping.

'Brave?' she jeered. 'You come after me wearing full armour, carrying a shield and a long sharp sword and you call yourself brave?'

'My true shield is Goodness!' said Sir Darryl. 'And my true sword is Justice! I just brought these others along in case.'

'And just how do you intend to vanquish me?' shrieked the Hag.

'I don't know,' confessed Sir Darryl. 'Nobody told me. I suppose I could lop off your head with one blow of my shining sword. That ought to do the trick!'

'Charming!' snapped the Hag. 'Then you pop my head into a sack and go running back to Camelot to show it off to all your knightly chums! Smashing Christmas I'm going to have this year!'

Sir Darryl was confused, cold and fed up. He forgot that knights of the Round Table were supposed to be polite to women and lost his temper.

'All right then, brain-box!' he fumed. 'You come up with a better suggestion!'

The Hag cackled and clapped her hands together. When her palms met, thunder boomed overhead.

'I'm a vile, evil-minded Hag,' she crowed, 'and you're a newly-made knight trying to prove your courage, right?'

'Right!' nodded Sir Darryl.

'Well then, my bold knight, let's see how brave you really are!' screeched the Hag. 'Take off your helmet, lay aside your shield and sword and . . .' She paused to cackle again.

'Yes?' asked Sir Darryl eagerly.

'Give us a kiss!' said the Hag.

'A kiss?' repeated Sir Darryl, amazed.

'I've never been kissed,' grumbled the Hag. 'Go on, give us one! It is Christmas. Look, I've brought a bit of mistletoe with me!'

The Hag held the mistletoe over her head and looked at Sir Darryl hopefully.

'I'm not sure I like the idea,' said Sir Darryl suspiciously. 'This could be a ruse! I smell an enchantment in the air.'

'Hah!' scoffed the Hag. 'Some big, brave knight you are! You'll chop the head off a poor, unarmed hag without batting an eyelid, but when it comes to one measly kiss under the mistletoe, you're a cowardy custard!'

Sir Darryl frowned uncertainly. 'You won't turn me into a newt, will you?'

'Cowardy custard!' sulked the Hag. 'I'm not sure I want you to kiss me now!'

Sir Darryl took off his helmet, placed his shield and sword on the ground beside it and approached the Hag cautiously.

'When did you last have a bath?' he asked.

'Don't be rude!' replied the Hag. 'If you're going to give me a kiss, get on with it and stop passing personal remarks!'

Trembling violently in every limb, Sir Darryl leaned forward, pressed his lips against the Hag's cheek and stood back at once.

The kiss left a small white patch on the Hag's cheek. As Sir Darryl watched, the white patch began to spread. The grime vanished from the Hag's face. Her hair untangled itself and billowed in glossy waves. The ragged black robe she wore was transformed into a green gown. In fact, the Hag became such a fair young maiden that Sir Darryl's breath was taken away.

'My bold knight!' said the maiden. 'You have freed me of the enchantment that was set upon me by the Awkward Witch of Oxford! I had almost given up hope that one day I would meet someone bold enough to kiss me and break the spell!'

'Gosh!' said Sir Darryl.

'My heart and hand are now yours!' said the maiden. 'I shall journey with you to Camelot and tell King Arthur of your courage.'

'Gosh!' said Sir Darryl.

'We shall eat spiced cakes and drink mulled wine and I shall dance every dance of the feasting with you, my bold knight!'

'Gosh!' said Sir Darryl.

The fair maiden frowned. 'Is that all you can say?' she asked.

'I'm more a man of action than words,' said Sir Darryl. 'But if you hold the mistle-toe up again, I wouldn't mind giving you another kiss!'

The fair maiden laughed. Her laugh was like all the Christmas bells of Camelot ringing in their steeples . . .

And she raised the mistletoe above her head.

Presents for Wrinklies

Every year, the Warrens went Christmas shopping together. On the last Saturday in November, the family drove into town and split up into two groups. Robert, Alice and Joan went in search of presents for their parents while Mum and Dad shopped for the children. Each group had a long list of possibilities provided by the other.

Robert, Alice and Joan made a beeline for Granville's Department Store and elbowed their way through the jostling crowds until they found an empty space in the Fabrics Department. The lengths of glittery, brightly coloured cloth surrounding them made it like being in an exotic jungle clearing. Robert and Alice looked through the list, Joan hopped and jerked to the music from her personal stereo.

'Scent, talcum powder, bath salts,' Robert read aloud, 'soap, deodorant, aftershave – '

'Aftershave?' Alice interrupted in astonishment.

'So it says here,' shrugged Robert.

'But Dad's got a beard!' frowned Alice. 'It must be awful, being old! Imagine having to use all that stuff to keep from smelling bad!'

Joan waved her hands above her head, chanting, 'Hey, bob-a-roonie! Chick, chick-a-boonie!'

Passing shoppers turned to stare and Alice blushed.

'She'll get us thrown out of here, I just know she will!' she hissed. 'Can't we sneak off and pretend she's not with us?'

Robert reached out and unplugged Alice's headphones. Alice scowled darkly at him.

'Oh, rat poo-plops!' she said loudly. 'It was just coming up to the best bit!'

'You can hear the rest when we get home,' said Robert. 'Right now we've got to concentrate on presents for Mum and Dad. What tape are you listening to, anyway?'

'Christmas carols!' replied Joan. 'Mega-wick! What do the wrinklies want this year?'

'The usual,' sighed Robert, passing Joan the list so that she could see for herself.

'Christabel Philbert's family is flying to Barbados this Christmas!' said Alice enviously. 'They're going to eat their roast turkey on a sun-kissed beach! We're going to be stuck at home with Uncle Kevin and Aunt Sandra!'

'Too right!' groaned Robert. 'Uncle Kevin will go on at Dad about not standing up for the Queen's Speech . . .'

'And Aunt Sandra will drink too much sherry and sing rude songs again!' moaned Alice.

'Ye-ukk!' yelled Joan. She was staring at the list, her face as wrinkled as a big toe that's been in the bath too long. 'These presents are crucially boring! Socks? Tights? Handkerchiefs? Gross!'

'It's not their fault,' said Alice. 'They're old and set in their ways, that's all. If we gave them interesting presents, they'd be over-excited and get indigestion.'

'And it's cruel to let Dad go on wearing those slippers he's got now,' Robert pointed out. 'They should have been put out of their misery years ago!'

Joan curled her top lip and stuck out her tongue.

'Change-a-roo time!' she growled. 'I'm not spending good money on this gank! I vote we get the old folks something super-maxi-surprising!'

'Such as?' enquired Robert.

A wicked smile stretched itself across Joan's mouth like a basking cat.

'Fee, fi, follow me!' she exclaimed.

Mum and Dad, meanwhile, were upstairs in Granville's Toy Department. Mum was consulting their list while Dad rummaged through a shelf of soft toys. He picked up a cuddly, pink pig with a bow of red ribbon around its neck and smiled.

'Isn't this cute?' he said. 'D'you think Alice would like this?'

'No,' said Mum. 'Alice wants a new horse-grooming set and a Pam Perks Pony Club Annual.'

'Oh!' said Dad. 'How about Joan, then? She'd love a cuddly pig!'

''Fraid not!' said Mum. 'She wants a bottle of Vampire Blood Bath Bubbles and an Alien Death-ray Robot.'

Dad looked crestfallen. He pressed the cuddly pig under the chin and made its snout twitch.

'We could get it as a silly present for Robert,' he suggested.

'Robert wants a pedal for his electric guitar,' said Mum, reading from the list.

'A pedal?' yelped Dad. 'What's he going to do with his guitar, ride it?'

'A pedal is a little box,' Mum explained. 'When Robert plugs his guitar into it, it changes the sound it makes. He says he's fed up with the guitar going jingle-jangle and wants something to make it go krank-kerbang.'

'Krank-kerbang?' gulped Dad. 'You mean we've got to go into the Music Department and ask for a pedal to make a guitar go krank-kerbang?'

'Robert's written the name of the pedal down,' said Mum. 'We ask for a Gritty Chicken. They'll know what we mean.'

Dad shook his head sadly and scratched the cuddly pig behind the left ear.

'Doesn't seem five minutes ago that we bought Robert his first train set, does it?' he said. 'Remember the year we got Alice her doll's house? And last Christmas, Joan wanted a – what was it again?'

'A Rat and Octopus Game,' said Mum. 'And she sulked because we forgot to buy batteries for it.'

'So,' said Dad glumly. 'No cuddly pig, then?'

'No cuddly pig,' said Mum.

Dad put the pig back on the shelf with the other soft toys.

'Shame, really,' he said quietly.

On Christmas morning, the Warrens gathered around the tree in their front room. It was Joan's turn to hand out the presents.

'I want to open this one now!' she cried, clutching a large parcel covered with silver paper.

'You know the rules!' said Dad sternly. 'All the presents have to be given out before anybody opens any of them.'

'Oh, hyena's knickers!' grumbled Joan. She passed the presents out at high speed, reading the labels and calling out, 'Rob-

bam-a-lam! Alice-a-boo! Mum-a-roonie! Pop-a-lop! Superlush me-me!'

'Suppose it isn't just a phase she's going through,' Dad muttered to Mum. 'Suppose she stays like this for the rest of her life!'

'Don't say that!' whispered Mum. 'You'll spoil Christmas for everybody!'

The next five minutes were chaos. Joan sprang on her presents like a starving tiger and disappeared behind a small blizzard of wrapping paper from which emerged shouts of, 'Crucial! Maxi-brill! Mega-ding-dong!'

Robert ripped open the tops of his presents, extracted the contents and said, 'Oh, wow! That's really cool!'

Alice teased the sellotape off her parcels and folded the wrapping paper into neat squares before examining her gifts. She kept on saying, 'Oh, how super!' as she always did when she was pleased.

'I suppose we'd better open ours as well,' said Dad wearily. 'Hardly seems worth it, really. When you've seen one pair of brown socks, you've seen them all.'

'Don't be such a misery!' said Mum. 'Open your biggest one and I'll open mine.'

Dad picked up a big red parcel and squeezed it gently.

'Slippers!' he grunted. 'Oh, well! I suppose I do need new ones.'

'Mine feels like a thermal vest!' said Mum unenthusiastically.

But it wasn't a thermal vest. It was a bright yellow jumper covered with purple kangaroos. Mum squealed with delight when she saw it and pulled it on over her dressing gown.

'You look ace!' yelled Joan.

'Wow!' exclaimed Robert. 'That's really cool!'

'Oh, how super!' breathed Alice, beaming at her mother.

Dad smiled to himself and tore open the wrapping on his present. It was a pink, cuddly pig with a bow of red ribbon around its neck. Dad's eyes bulged and his mouth fell open.

'Well?' demanded Joan.

'Do you like it?' Alice asked anxiously.

'What d'you reckon, Dad?' said Robert.

Dad held the pig close to his face and pressed the tip of his nose against its snout.

'I reckon it's super-mega-brill!' he said.

Hecate's Midnight Hamper

It was the day after Boxing Day. Elizabeth and Brian Bayliss were sitting on the sofa in the front room. They were supposed to be watching television, but Elizabeth was reading a comic annual for the third time and Brian was scribbling in the back of a diary Aunt Tracy had sent him. The television was on, showing the same film that had been shown on the day after Boxing Day three years in a row. The front sitting-room door was open, and through it wafted the clanking sounds of Mum and Dad preparing lunch.

'What d'you think lunch will be, Bri?' Elizabeth asked idly.

'I'm working it out,' said Brian. 'Roast turkey on Christmas Day, turkey sandwiches for Christmas supper. Yesterday it was turkey curry and then turkey royale. So, I reckon that for lunch today we'll have turkey something-or-other.'

Elizabeth dropped her annual on to the carpet and sighed loudly.

'I hate this part of Christmas!' she grumbled. 'I'm bored with all the toys, we've read all the books and played all the games. We can't use any of the gift tokens we've

got because the shops aren't open and we've seen all the TV programmes before! I've had four baths in the last two days so I could try out all my bath salts!'

'And I,' said Brian, reading from the scribbles in his diary, 'have eaten twenty-seven mince pies, eight ounces of plum pudding, two selection boxes, fifteen walnuts, four oranges and three pieces of Christmas cake. And did you know that if you had a lump of iron the same weight as all the turkey I've eaten, you'd have enough to make a fair-sized cannonball?'

'I'll go bonkers if I don't do something!' moaned Elizabeth. 'If Dad says "must be nice, sitting around doing nothing all day" once more, I'll scream!'

'There is one present I haven't used yet . . .' said Brian thoughtfully.

Before Elizabeth could ask what, Dad put his head around the door and announced, 'Lunch! Turkey Hawaii, with pineapple and cherries. Look lively, you two! Must be nice, sitting around doing nothing all day!'

Elizabeth's scream knocked the star off the top of the Christmas tree.

*

Elizabeth got ten metres up the back lane and stopped walking.

'It's no good, Bri!' she said. 'I feel a right dimlow! Dragging a sled behind us would make sense if there was any snow about! But look!' Elizabeth held out her arms to show Brian the damp hedges and watery sun. 'We had days in summer that were colder than this!'

Brian blushed and scraped the toe of one of his trainers along the cinder path.

'All right,' he said, 'I admit we do look like a couple of wallies with the sled, but it's got us out of the house, hasn't it?'

'I suppose so,' shrugged Elizabeth. 'But going out for a walk isn't exactly the most exciting thing in the world, is it?'

'Let's walk down the footpath across the fields,' suggested Brian.

'Great!' snapped Elizabeth. 'We can have a cowpat counting competition!'

Getting the sled over the stile into the field proved tricky, but Elizabeth and Brian managed it at last.

The field was a raggedy, bumpy, sad-looking piece of ground.

'Hello!' said Brian. 'What's that?'

'It's a field, Bri!'

'I meant that over there, numbskull!' said Brian, pointing.

'Twenty metres away from the children, something was lying at the foot of a hawthorn hedge.

'Looks like a box,' said Elizabeth sulkily.

'Let's take a closer look!'

Reluctantly, Elizabeth slouched along beside her brother. As they drew closer to the hedge, however, her curiosity was pricked.

It was a hamper, not a box; a proper wicker hamper, with leather straps and a label on the lid.

HECATE'S MIDNIGHT HAMPER
BUMPER CHRISTMAS SPECIAL

'There's a gift card on the handle,' said Elizabeth, turning it over to read. 'From Goody Screechworthy to Goody Charmnasty.' She looked at Brian and frowned. 'That's a bit weird, isn't it?'

Brian was thinking. He held his chin with his left hand, the way that Dad did.

'This is someone else's property,' he said slowly. 'Strictly speaking, we should take it home with us and call the police. It would be really, really wrong to open it and take a look inside.'

'You're absolutely right, Bri!' said Elizabeth. 'You undo the right strap and I'll undo the left one, OK?'

The left strap unbuckled easily enough, but the right one wouldn't budge – even when Elizabeth and Brian tugged at it together.

'I've got thin hands!' said Elizabeth. 'I could reach in and get some stuff out.' Brian gave her a stern frown. 'Only for a look, Bri! I'll put them straight back afterwards!'

'All right, then!' mumbled Brian. He didn't feel too happy about it, but it was more interesting than sitting in front of the television.

Elizabeth slipped her hand under the lid. At once, her fingers closed around something cold and square.

'I think it's a tin!' she cried. She squeezed the tin out under the lid and examined it carefully.

'What's in it?' Brian asked.

Elizabeth screwed up her face in disappointment.

'Baby powder!' she groaned. 'A tin of baby powder! Big deal!'

'Let's have a look,' said Brian.

'I thought things were getting really interesting for a minute!' Elizabeth complained. 'And then I find myself holding a tin of baby powder. Wow! Stupendous! A thrill in a million!'

'Er . . . Liz,' said Brian. 'Have you read this bit underneath where it says "Baby Powder"?'

'What bit?'

'This bit,' said Brian, pointing to the label.

DAGON BRAND BABY POWDER

JUST ADD WATER

'Just add water?' Elizabeth exclaimed. 'What does that mean?'

'Haven't got a clue,' said Brian. He opened the plastic screwcap on top of the tin and sniffed curiously.

A hideous smell made Brian sneeze. As he sneezed, he dropped the tin and some white powder fell on to the damp grass.

'Bri-an!' wailed Elizabeth.

The powder was hissing and fizzing,

making bubbles that grew bigger and bigger until – POP! – a huge one burst and there was a pink baby wriggling in the grass and then – POP! – there was another and – POP! – another and – POP! POP! POP!

'No' shouted Brian. 'Oh, dear! You mustn't!'

Elizabeth stared, open-mouthed.

By the time the powder stopped fizzing, there were thirteen babies kicking and struggling in the grass. They were all unhappy and they were all bawling at the tops of their tiny lungs.

'Where did they come from?' gasped Brian.

'Never mind that!' replied Elizabeth. 'Now they're here, what on earth are we going to do with them?'

Brian flapped his arms helplessly. 'Um, they need to have their nappies changed and then we should feed them and put them to bed.'

'Brian,' said Elizabeth patiently, 'we can't change their nappies because they aren't wearing any. Even if we take them home we haven't got thirteen beds to put them in!'

'Well, at least let's feed them!' said Brian tetchily. 'Anything, so long as we get them to shut up!'

'Feed them with what?'

'Maybe there's something in the hamper! That's where the baby powder came from, after all!'

Elizabeth tiptoed carefully through the babies and stuck her hand under the lid of the hamper. This time, she brought out a large plastic tub.

CHOCOLATE MOOSE
MADE IN CANADA

'Funny!' thought Elizabeth. 'Shouldn't it be spelled . . . ?'

'Hurry up!' yelled Brian, holding his hands over his ears. 'I'm going deaf!'

Elizabeth pulled the lid off the tub. Brown fur, hooves and enormous antlers poured out of it and assembled themselves into a fully grown, milk chocolate moose.

Elizabeth opened her mouth to speak, but all that would come out was, 'Bip!'

'Hi there!' boomed the moose in a Canadian accent. 'My name's Mack Moose and I'd just like to say how wonderful it is to be with you right here in the old UK! Say, I'm feeling mighty hungry after my trip and I was wondering if I could use your phone to order a pepperoni and maple syrup pizza? Or maybe I could fix myself a boysenberry and Arctic moss open sandwich? Boy, it's pretty warm over here! Back in Canada, it's twenty below and that can cause some problems when you're a moose! Take going to the bathroom, for instance . . .' Mack Moose launched into a detailed and disgusting description.

'Argh!' screamed Brian. 'Thirteen bawling babies and a motor-mouth moose made of chocolate! I can't stand it! I'm cracking up!'

He rushed over to the hamper and thrust his hand inside. Brian's hand was bigger

than Elizabeth's and he skimmed his knuckles on the wickerwork as he yanked it free. He was holding an old fashioned cut-glass scent bottle with a bulb and tube fitted to a nozzle at the top. The bottle was labelled:

OLD FAMILIAR
ONE PRESS, THEN STAND WELL BACK
EMERGENCY USE ONLY

'This is an emergency, all right!' said Brian grimly and he gave the bulb a hard squeeze.

A dark mist hissed out of the nozzle and hung in the air, curling and coiling over itself until it turned solid and became a cat.

The cat was in a seated position, was jet black and was the size of a Shetland pony. It took one look at Brian and Elizabeth, flattened its ears and hissed angrily.

'What's this? You're not Sisters of the Moon! What do you children think you're up to, meddling with magic?'

'W-we d-didn't mean to!' trembled Brian. 'We were out for a walk when we found this hamper and . . .'

'Don't tell me Goody Screechworthy dropped something off her broomstick again!' growled the cat. 'We keep telling her to use the post, but she's too mean to buy stamps!'

'A-W-A-A-A-R-G-H!' screamed the babies.

'Now,' Mack Moose rabbited on, 'you might think eating lichen and tree bark would come naturally to a moose. But I'll bet you didn't know the effect those things have on a moose's insides. Let me tell you about it! First of all – '

'Can you help us?' Elizabeth shouted to

the cat. 'We seem to have got ourselves into a bit of a mess!'

The cat looked at the babies, shuddered, looked at Mack Moose and shuddered again.

'So it seems!' it said. 'I think you two had better shut your eyes for a moment.'

'Why?' asked Elizabeth.

'It will save you having bad dreams for the rest of your life,' the cat replied.

Elizabeth and Brian closed their eyes tightly. At once, a bright red light pressed against their eyelids and there was a rumbling that made the ground shake. Then the light went out, the rumbling stopped and there was silence.

Gingerly, Elizabeth and Brian opened their eyes. No babies, no chocolate moose, no cat. The hamper had sprouted bright

yellow chicken legs and was belting off across the field at remarkable speed. The children watched it until it cleared a hawthorn hedge with one jump and was lost to view.

They were quiet for a long time afterwards. Brian tried to think of what to say. After what had happened, what could he say? At last, he made up his mind. He cleared his throat and said, 'D'you know what I reckon, Liz?'

'What, Bri?'

'I reckon we'll have cold turkey and chips for tea tonight,' said Brian.

And a Partridge in a Pear Tree

It was Christmas Eve and Prince Truelove was terribly nervous. He paced the Royal Chamber restlessly, or gazed anxiously at the logs blazing in the Royal Hearth. Outside in the courtyard, a choir sang carols, but the Prince hardly heard a note. All he could hear was Princess Debbie's voice and when he looked into the fire the glowing embers seemed to form the shape of her face. In fact, the Prince was so deep in daydreams about the Princess that he did not notice the Royal Chamberlain enter the room.

'A-hem!' the Chamberlain coughed discreetly. 'I have brought a map of the procession for your perusal, Your Highness!'

Eagerly, the Prince examined the unrolled parchment. A concerned look crossed his face.

'Look here!' he cried, pointing. 'There's a place called "Troll Bridge". There's a picture of a troll next to it – and next to the troll there's some writing that says "Beware of the Troll". What does all this mean, Chamberlain?'

'It means that a troll lives under the bridge, Your Highness,' the Chamberlain replied.

'B-but trolls . . . eat people, don't they?' shuddered the Prince.

'That is their custom, I believe, Your Highness,' said the Chamberlain calmly,

'but to take any other road would add a day to the journey. Besides, it is a well-known fact that trolls sleep through the winter months.'

The Prince looked relieved at this news, then started pacing up and down again.

'I'm sure that my Christmas present will please Princess Debbie so much, she'll marry me at once!' he said. 'Is everything exactly as I explained?'

'Not . . . exactly, Your Highness,' said the Chamberlain gravely. 'The swans, geese, colly birds and French hens are just as you required. The Royal Gamekeeper has succeeded in training a partridge to stay in a pear tree. The Royal Goldsmith has made five exceptionally beautiful rings, inscribed as you requested. The milkmaids, drummers and dancing ladies are ready and waiting . . . only . . .'

'What?' demanded the Prince.

'The leaping lords, Your Highness. Only eleven remain,' admitted the Chamberlain. 'There were twelve originally, but Lord McSnurt has come down with gout and there isn't a leap left in him.'

The Prince began to tear at his hair.

'Only eleven?' he groaned. 'That ruins everything! How can I send her eleven leaping lords on the twelfth day of Christmas? It'll look so stupid!'

'I'm sure that eleven will prove to be sufficient acrobatic aristocracy, Your Highness,' murmured the Chamberlain.

From a far corner of the room came the chiming of the Royal Clock.

'Well, it's too late now!' snapped the Prince. 'Eleven will have to do. But if it doesn't work, I shall blame you, Chamberlain. If Princess Debbie turns me down, I shall have your beard plucked out with tweezers!'

'Ah!' sighed the Chamberlain. 'What it is to be young, and in love!'

The procession set off at one-thirty exactly. The Prince had intended the journey to be a dignified affair, but it did not turn out quite as he had imagined. The French hens and colly birds squawked and whistled, the swans and geese hissed, the milkmaids giggled and the cows mooed loudly. Then came the drummers, the pipers, the dancing ladies and the leaping lords who, as they leapt, shouted, 'Whee!' and 'Boing!' and 'Yippee!' All the sounds together made an awful racket.

At the front of the procession, the Prince leaned across his horse and tugged the Chamberlain's sleeve.

'It's a bit noisy, isn't it?' he yelled. 'Perhaps I should have stuck to quiet presents, like the five gold rings!'

'I'm sure Princess Debbie will be quite charmed, Your Highness,' smiled the Chamberlain.

The procession was so loud that people could hear it a mile off and they gathered at the roadside to stare in open-mouthed wonder. Prince Truelove felt embarrassed, but the thought of Princess Debbie's flashing eyes gave him the courage to go on.

The road threaded its way through a wood, then steepened as it climbed up to a narrow mountain pass. The noise of the procession echoed and re-echoed off the sides of the mountains until the Prince's head began to ache and spin.

'I can't stand it!' he groaned.

'Take heart, Your Highness!' urged the Chamberlain. 'See, a short way ahead lies Troll Bridge! It's all downhill after that!'

Troll Bridge spanned a deep chasm. Far below it, a mountain torrent raged its way around huge, jagged boulders. Prince Truelove, who was not fond of heights, shut his eyes and gripped his reins tightly.

No sooner had his horse taken one step on to the bridge than there came the sound of a bellow so loud that the entire procession fell silent.

'Oi!' bawled a voice. 'What's all the row about?'

The Prince opened his eyes wide. To his horror, an enormous and fearsomely ugly troll clambered up on to the far end of the bridge, blocking the way.

'What's this lot, then?' roared the troll. 'Ain't you got no consideration? You've disturbed me 'ibernation!' The troll drew a spiked club from his belt and tested the sharpness of the spikes against his thumb.

'Troll!' called the Prince. 'This procession is my Christmas present to Princess Debbie and – '

'Why didn't you buy 'er a new dress or a box o' chocolates like anyone else would?' scoffed the troll.

'And,' continued the Prince, ignoring the troll's interruption, 'if you don't stand aside immediately, I shall . . . I shall . . .'

'Yeah?' said the troll.

'You will incur the Royal Displeasure,' said the Chamberlain, 'and a proclamation about you will be read aloud in every village!'

''Ow terrible!' laughed the troll. 'Why, I'm tremblin' in me boots at the very idea!' He pointed his club straight at the Prince. 'You look like you'd make a tasty suet

puddin', me lad!' he growled. 'And as for you,' he squinted at the Chamberlain, 'you look a bit on the tough side. I think I'll pickle you for later! Now I'm awake, I could just do with a toothsome trollish snack!'

The troll began to cross the bridge.

'Chamberlain!' squeaked the Prince. 'Think of something!'

'I am sorely tempted to suggest that we flee faster than the wind, Your Highness,' said the Chamberlain, 'but I fear that trolls are well known for their athletic prowess.'

And that gave the Prince a splendid idea. He looked the troll squarely in the face and said loudly, 'Can you run?'

The troll found the question so astonishing that he stood still in the middle of the bridge.

'Run?' he frowned. 'Course I can run! Gotta keep fit in my game, y'know! You'd be amazed 'ow fast people goes when they got an 'ungry troll be'ind 'em!'

'And how about swimming?' asked the Prince hurriedly.

'Like a fish!' said the troll proudly.

'But can you leap?' Prince Truelove enquired.

'Watch this!' said the troll. He tucked his club back under his belt, crouched for a second and then performed the most tremendous backwards somersault, landing on the far side of the chasm.

The milkmaids, ladies and lords burst into applause and the troll bowed.

'Piece o' cake!' he mumbled. 'No, really, it was nothin'!'

Just before the applause died down, the Prince raised his hand for silence.

'I've got an offer you can't refuse,' he told the troll. 'I'm a leaping lord short and you seem to have a talent for leaping. If you'll join the procession, I'll make you a lord!'

'Well, well!' gasped the troll, scratching his head. 'Me, a lord! Cor, that'd be somethin' to tell the other trolls, wouldn't it?' A cunning gleam came into his eyes. 'What about me ravenous 'unger, then?'

'Fear not!' exclaimed the Chamberlain. 'For, where we are bound, a sumptuous feast of delicate dainties awaits!'

'Eh?' puzzled the troll.

'We're goin' to a knees-up!' shouted one of the pipers. 'There'll be plenty o' posh nosh!'

'Sounds dead wicked!' rumbled the troll, smacking his lips. 'OK, it's a deal!'

'Kneel down and I shall dub you!' Prince Truelove commanded. He rode across the bridge to where the troll waited, sunk down on to one knee. Even so, he was as tall as the Prince's horse. Prince Truelove drew his sword and touched the flat of the blade on the troll's shoulder. 'Arise . . . er, what's your name?'

'Doug,' said the troll.

'Arise, Lord Doug!' proclaimed the Prince.

And in the end, it was Lord Doug who did the trick. For, as Princess Debbie explained to her lady-in-waiting later, any Prince who went to the trouble of taming a troll as a Christmas present must be suffering from a bad attack of true love.

In fact, the Prince's attack of true love was so bad that it spread. The eleven leaping lords proposed to the dancing ladies and were accepted. All the drummers and the pipers who were not already married found themselves betrothed to the milkmaids. Everybody decided that they would wed on the same day as Prince Truelove and Princess Debbie.

As for Lord Doug, he went back to the mountains to finish his hibernation. But the following spring, he awoke a changed troll. He gave up eating people completely and turned vegetarian.

'Well, it's like this,' he said, when any of his fellow trolls asked him about it. 'I'm a lord now. I got me dignity to think of, ain't I? When you're a member of the upper class, you can't be caught eatin' riff-raff, mate!'

Also available from Andrew Matthews

WOLF PIE

What happens when a cruel and greedy King and queen order a dish they have never eaten before? Who ends up in a barrel of jellyfish? Why do the Apprentice Chefs run away? And what have wolves got to do with it?

If your taste is for stories which are funny (and a bit rude!) open up this pie and discover its very strange contents . . .

DIXIE'S DEMON

When your pet is small and a bit on the fiendish side, Dixie discovers, you get an awful lot of hassle. You get into trouble with your parents, your friends laugh at you and the biggest yobbo in school wants to duff you up. Added to which, demons have some . . . well . . . peculiar personal habits.

A very funny story of one boy and his demon.

THE QUIET PIRATE

'Yo ho ho and a cup of tea.
A pirate's life is not for me!'

William Barrett counts all the peas in the Kingdom of Dunroamin. He is quite happy until his swashbuckling uncle whisks him away one day to turn him into a pirate. Before long, William and his cat are mixed up with a cowardly Duke, a stubborn Princess and the barmiest crew of bungling pirates ever to sail the seven seas!

A Selected List of Titles Available from Mammoth

While every effort is made to keep prices low, it is sometimes necessary to increase prices at short notice. Mammoth Paperbacks reserves the right to show new retail prices on covers which may differ from those previously advertised in the text or elsewhere.

The prices shown below were correct at the time of going to press.

☐	416 96490 7	**Dilly the Dinosaur**	Tony Bradman	£1.99
☐	749 70166 8	**The Witch's Big Toe**	Ralph Wright	£1.75
☐	416 95910 5	**The Grannie Season**	Joan Phipson	£1.75
☐	416 58270 2	**Listen to this Story**	Grace Hallworth	£1.75
☐	416 10382 0	**The Knights of Hawthorn Crescent**	Jenny Koralek	£1.50
☐	416 13882 5	**It's Abigail Again**	Moira Miller	£1.99
☐	749 70218 4	**Lucy Jane at the Ballet**	Susan Hampshire	£1.50
☐	416 06432 9	**Alf Gorilla**	Michael Grater	£1.75
☐	416 10362 6	**Owl and Billy**	Martin Waddell	£1.50
☐	416 13122 0	**Hetty Pegler, Half-Witch**	Margaret Greaves	£1.75
☐	749 70137 4	**Flat Stanley**	Jeff Brown	£1.99
☐	416 00572 1	**Princess Polly to the Rescue**	Mary Lister	£1.50
☐	416 00552 7	**Non Stop Nonsense**	Margaret Mahy	£1.75
☐	416 10322 7	**Claudius Bald Eagle**	Sam McBratney	£1.75
☐	416 03212 5	**I Don't Want To!**	Bel Mooney	£1.99

All these books are available at your bookshop or newsagent, or can be ordered direct from the publisher. Just tick the titles you want and fill in the form below.

Mammoth Paperbacks, Cash Sales Department, PO Box 11, Falmouth, Cornwall TR10 9EN.

Please send cheque or postal order, no currency, for purchase price quoted and allow the following for postage and packing:

UK	55p for the first book, 22p for the second book and 14p for each additional book ordered to a maximum charge of £1.75.
BFPO and Eire	55p for the first book, 22p for the second book and 14p for each of the next seven books, thereafter 8p per book.
Overseas Customers	£1.00 for the first book plus 25p per copy for each additional book.

NAME (Block letters) ....

ADDRESS ....

....